To the fairies at the bottom
of my garden

Special thanks to
Narinder Dhami

ORCHARD BOOKS

First published in Great Britain in 2003 by Orchard Books
This edition published in 2017 by The Watts Publishing Group

34

Copyright © 2017 Rainbow Magic Limited.
Copyright © 2017 HIT Entertainment Limited.
Illustrations copyright © Georgie Ripper, 2003

HIT entertainment

A CIP catalogue record for this book is available from the British Library.

ISBN 978 1 84362 019 8

Printed and bound in Great Britain by Clays Ltd, Elcograf S.p.A.

MIX
Paper from
responsible sources
FSC® C104740

The paper and board used in this book are made from wood from responsible sources

Orchard Books
An imprint of Hachette Children's Group
Part of The Watts Publishing Group Limited
Carmelite House, 50 Victoria Embankment, London EC4Y 0DZ

An Hachette UK Company
www.hachette.co.uk
www.hachettechildrens.co.uk

Fern
the Green
Fairy

Join the Rainbow Magic Reading Challenge!

Read the story and collect your fairy points to climb the
Reading Rainbow at the back of the book.

This book is worth 5 points.

Cold winds blow and thick ice form,
I conjure up this fairy storm.
To seven corners of the mortal world
the Rainbow Fairies will be hurled!

I curse every part of Fairyland,
with a frosty wave of my icy hand.
For now and always, from this fateful day,
Fairyland will be cold and grey!

Ruby, Amber and Saffron
are out of danger.
Will Rachel and Kirsty free
Fern the **Green Fairy** too?

Contents

The Secret Garden 9

Where is Fern? 19

Lost in the Maze 29

Fairy Fireworks 39

Hedgehog Help 57

Flying High 67

The Secret Garden

"Oh!" Rachel Walker gasped in delight, as she gazed around her. "What a perfect place for a picnic!"

"It's a secret garden," Kirsty Tate said, her eyes shining.

They were standing in a large garden. It looked as if nobody else had been there for a long, long time.

Pink and white roses grew all around
the tree trunks, filling the air with sweet
perfume. White marble statues stood
here and there, half hidden by trailing,
green ivy. And right in the middle of
the garden was a crumbling stone
tower.

"There was a castle here once called
Moonspinner Castle," Mr Walker said,
looking at his guidebook. "But now all
that's left is the tower."

Rachel and Kirsty stared up at the ruined tower. The yellow stones glowed warmly in the sunshine. They were covered in soft, green moss. Near the top of the tower was a small, square window.

"It's just like Rapunzel's tower," Kirsty said. "I wonder if we can get up to the top?"

"Let's go and see!" Rachel said eagerly. "I want to explore the whole garden. Can we, Mum?"

"Off you go," smiled Mrs Walker. "Your dad and I will get the food ready." She opened the picnic basket. "But don't be too long, girls."

Rachel and Kirsty rushed over to the door in the side of the tower. Kirsty tugged at the heavy iron handle. But the door was locked.

Rachel felt disappointed. "Oh, that's a shame," she said.

Kirsty sighed. "Yes, I was hoping Fern the Green Fairy might be here."

Rachel and Kirsty had a secret. They were helping to find the seven Rainbow Fairies before the end of their holiday on Rainspell Island. The fairies had been cast out of Fairyland by evil Jack Frost, and Fairyland had lost all its colour. Only when all seven fairies returned home would Fairyland be bright and beautiful again.

"Fern," Rachel called in a low voice. "Are you here?"

Here... Here... Here...

Her words echoed off the stones. Rachel and Kirsty held their breath and waited. But they couldn't hear anything except leaves rustling in the breeze.

13

"It's such a special place," Kirsty said. "It *feels* like there's magic close by." Then she gasped and pointed. "Rachel, look at the ivy!"

Rachel stared. Glossy green leaves grew thickly on the wall, but in one place the stones were bare, in the shape of a perfect circle.

Rachel's heart began to beat faster. "It's just like a fairy ring!" she said. She ran round the tower to take a closer look, and almost tripped over the lace of one of her trainers.

"Careful!" Kirsty said, grabbing Rachel's arm.

Rachel sat down on a mossy stone to retie her shoelace. "There's green *everywhere*," she said, looking round at the lush grass and the leafy trees. "Fern *must* be here."

"We'd better find her quickly then," Kirsty said with a shiver. "In case Jack Frost's goblins find her first!"

15

Jack Frost had sent his goblin servants to Rainspell. He wanted them to stop the fairies from getting home to Fairyland.

"Where shall we start looking?" Rachel asked, standing up again.

Kirsty laughed. "You've got green stuff all over you!" she said.

Rachel twisted round to look. The back of her denim skirt was green and dusty. "It must be the moss," she grumbled, brushing it off.

The dust flew up into the air. It sparkled and glittered in the morning sun. As it fell to the ground, tiny, green leaves appeared and the smell of freshly cut grass filled the air.

Rachel and Kirsty turned to each other. "It's fairy dust!" they gasped together.

Where is Fern?

"Fern *is* here!" said Kirsty.

"Thank goodness I sat down on that fairy dust!" Rachel said.

They walked all round the tower, looking under bushes and inside sweet-smelling flowers. As they walked, they softly called Fern's name. But the Green Fairy was nowhere to be found.

19

"You don't think the goblins have caught her, do you?" Rachel said, feeling very worried.

"I hope not," replied Kirsty. "I'm sure Fern *was* here, but now she's somewhere else."

"Yes, but where?" Rachel looked round the garden in despair.

"Maybe there's magic around to help us," Kirsty said hopefully.

She looked down at the tiny leaves. Some of them had begun to flutter across the garden. "I know, let's follow the fairy dust."

The bright green leaves floated over to a narrow path that led into a beautiful orchard. Rachel could see apples, pears and plums growing on the trees.

"It's a magic trail!" Kirsty breathed.

"Quick, let's keep following the fairy dust," Rachel said.

Rachel and Kirsty set off along the path, which twisted and turned through the fruit trees.

Suddenly the path opened out into a large clearing. Kirsty's eyes opened wide when she saw what was in front of them. "It's a maze!" she cried.

The thick, green hedges loomed above them, their leaves rustling softly.

Rachel nudged Kirsty. "Look," she pointed. "The fairy trail goes right into the maze!"

"We'll have to follow it," Kirsty said bravely.

The two girls followed the floating fairy leaves through the narrow entrance. Kirsty felt a bit scared as the fairy dust led them first one way, then another between the green hedges. What if the trail ran out and they got lost in the maze?

"Maybe there'll be another clue in the middle of the maze," Rachel said hopefully.

"Or maybe Fern will be there!" Kirsty added.

They turned one more corner and suddenly the hedges parted to reveal the centre of the maze. A nut tree stood in the very middle. The fairy dust led right to the bottom of the tree, then stopped.

"Fern must be here!" Rachel said excitedly.

Kirsty frowned. "Yes, but *where*?" she asked, looking round.

Tap! Tap! Tap!
The two girls jumped.
"What was that?" Rachel gasped.

There it was again. *Tap! Tap! Tap!*
Kirsty's eyes opened wide. "It's coming from over there." She pointed at the nut tree.

"I hope it isn't a goblin trap," Rachel whispered.

Tap! Tap! Tap!

The noise was louder now. Slowly
Rachel and Kirsty walked right round
the tree. At first they couldn't see
anything unusual.

Then Rachel pointed at the trunk.
"What's a *window* doing in a *tree*?"
she gasped.

There was a small, hollow knot
halfway up the trunk – and it was
covered by a glass window!

Kirsty put out her hand and touched
the window. It was very cold and wet.
"It's not glass," she whispered. "It's *ice*!"

Both girls looked more closely.
Suddenly, something moved behind the
icy window. Kirsty could just make out
a tiny girl dressed in glittering green.

"Rachel, we've found her!" she said
happily. "It's Fern, the Green Fairy!"

Lost in the Maze

Fern waved to the girls through the sheet of ice. Her mouth opened and closed, but Rachel and Kirsty couldn't hear a word she was saying. The ice was too thick.

Rachel looked worried. "She must be freezing in there," she said. "We've got to get her out."

"We could smash the ice with a stick," said Kirsty. Then she frowned. "But Fern might get hurt."

Rachel thought hard. "We could *melt* the ice," she said.

"How?" Kirsty asked.

"Like this," Rachel replied. She reached up and pressed her hand firmly against the window of ice. Kirsty did the same. The ice felt freezing cold, but they kept on pressing against it with their warm hands.

30

Soon, a few drops of water began to trickle down the window.

"It's melting!" Rachel said. "We can make a hole in it now." She gently poked the middle of the window with her finger, and the ice began to crack.

"Don't worry, Fern," cried Kirsty. "You'll be out of there very soon!"

There was a sudden crack, as the ice
split open. A flash of sparkling fairy
dust shot out, leaving behind a lovely
scent of cut grass. And then Fern
the Green Fairy pushed her
way out of the icy
window, her wings
fluttering limply. She
wore a bright green
top and stretchy
trousers, with pretty
leaf shapes round her
waist and neck. She had
small, green pixie boots on her
tiny feet, and earrings and a pendant
that looked like a little, green leaf.
Her long, brown hair was tied in
bunches, and her slender, emerald
wand was tipped with gold.

"Oh, I'm s–s–so c–c–cold!" the fairy gasped, shivering all over. She floated down to rest on Kirsty's shoulder.

"Let me warm you up a bit," said Rachel. She scooped the fairy up and held her in her cupped hands. Then she blew gently on her.

The warmth of Rachel's breath seemed to do the trick. Fern stopped shivering, and her wings straightened out. "Thank you," she said. "I feel much better now."

"I'm Rachel and this is Kirsty,"
Rachel explained. "We're here to take
you to the pot-at-the-end-
of-the-rainbow."

"Ruby, Amber
and Saffron
are waiting
for you,"
Kirsty added.
Fern's green
eyes lit up.
"They're safe!"
she exclaimed.
"That's wonderful!"
She flew off Rachel's
hand in a blaze of green
fairy dust and twirled joyfully
in the air. "But what about my other
sisters?"

"Don't worry, we're going to find them too," Kirsty told her. "How did you get stuck behind the ice window?"

"When I landed on Rainspell Island, I got tangled up in the ivy on the tower," Fern explained. "I managed to untangle myself, but then Jack Frost's goblins started chasing me. So I ran into the maze and hid in the nut tree. But it was raining, and when the goblins passed by, the rainwater turned to ice. So I was trapped."

Suddenly Rachel shivered. "It's getting colder," she said. She glanced up at the sky. The sun had disappeared behind a cloud, and there was a sudden chill in the air.

"The goblins must be close by!"
Kirsty gasped, looking scared.

Fern nodded. "Yes, we'd better get
out of this garden right away," she
said calmly. "You know the way,
don't you?"

Rachel and Kirsty looked at each
other.

"I'm not sure," Kirsty said with a
frown. "Do *you* know, Rachel?"

Rachel shook her head. "No," she
replied. "But we can follow the fairy
trail back to the start of the maze."

Kirsty looked around. "Where *is* the
fairy trail?" she asked.

An icy breeze was blowing all around
them now. The green fairy leaves were
drifting away and vanishing in front of
their very eyes.

"Oh no!" Kirsty gasped. "What are we going to do now?"

Suddenly they heard the sound of heavy footsteps coming through the maze towards them.

"I know that fairy is in here *somewhere* ," grumbled a loud, gruff voice.

Fern, Rachel and Kirsty stared at each other in dismay.

"Goblins!" whispered Rachel.

Fairy Fireworks

Rachel, Kirsty and Fern listened in horror as the goblins came closer. As usual, they were arguing with each other.

"Come on!" snorted one goblin. "We can't let her get away again."

"Stop bossing me about," whined the other one. "I'm going as fast as I can. OW!"

There was a loud *THUD!* It sounded as if the goblin had fallen over.

"If your feet weren't so big, you wouldn't trip over them," jeered the first goblin.

"They're big enough to give you a good kick!" the other goblin snapped.

"Let's hide in the tree," Fern whispered to Rachel and Kirsty. "I'll make you fairy-sized, so we can all fit under a leaf." Quickly she shot up into the air and sprinkled the girls with fairy dust. Rachel and Kirsty gasped as they felt themselves shrinking, down and down.

It was so exciting!

Fern took the girls' hands. "Let's go," she said, and the three of them fluttered up into the air and landed on a branch.

Fat brown hazelnuts grew on the tree, as big as beachballs. Even the thinnest twigs looked like tree trunks to the tiny girls! Fern heaved up the edge of a leaf, which was as big as a tablecloth, and they all crept underneath.

A moment later, the goblins rushed into the clearing.

"Where can that fairy be?" grumbled one of them. "I know she came this way!"

They began to search around the bottom of the tree.

"How are we going to get back to the pot?" Rachel whispered to Fern.

Fern laughed. "Don't worry! I think I know someone who can help us!" And she pointed past them.

Rachel and Kirsty turned to look.
A furry, grey face was peeping shyly
round the tree trunk. It was a squirrel.

"Hello," Fern called softly.

The squirrel jumped and hid behind
the trunk. Then he peeped out again,
his dark eyes curious.

"Maybe he'd like a hazelnut?"
Kirsty suggested.

There was a big, shiny nut growing
right next to her. She
wrapped her arms around
it, but she couldn't pull
it off the twig. Rachel
and Fern came to
help. All three of
them tugged at the
nut until it came off
the branch with a jump.

Fern held it out to the squirrel. "Mmm, a yummy nut!" she said.

The squirrel ran lightly along the branch, his long, furry tail waving. He took the hazelnut and held it in his front paws.

"What's your name?" asked Fern kindly.

"I'm Fluffy," squeaked the squirrel, between nibbles.

"I'm Fern," said the fairy. "And these are my friends, Rachel and Kirsty. We need to get away from the goblins. Will you help us?"

Fluffy shivered. "I don't like goblins," he squeaked.

"We won't let them hurt you," Fern promised, stroking his head. "Can you give us a ride on your back? You can jump from hedge to hedge much better than we can! We have to get out of the maze."

"Yes, I'll help you," Fluffy agreed, finishing the last piece of nut.

Rachel, Kirsty and Fern climbed on to the squirrel's back. Kirsty thought it was just like sinking into a big, soft blanket.

"This is lovely," said Fern, snuggling down into the squirrel's fur. "Let's go, Fluffy!"

The squirrel turned and ran along the branch. Rachel, Kirsty and Fern clung tightly to Fluffy's thick fur as he jumped out of the tree, right over the goblins' heads! He landed neatly on the nearest hedge. The goblins were so busy arguing, they didn't even notice.

Fern leaned forward to whisper in the squirrel's ear. "Well done, Fluffy. Now the next one!"

Rachel gulped when she saw how far away the next hedge was. "Maybe Fluffy needs some fairy magic to help him," she said.

"No, he doesn't," Fern replied, her green eyes twinkling. "He'll be fine!"

Fluffy leaped into mid-air. He sailed across the gap and landed safely on top of the next hedge. Rachel and Kirsty grinned at each other. This was so exciting! It was a bit bumpy, but Fluffy's fur was like a soft cushion. The squirrel was moving so fast, it wasn't long before they had left the goblins far behind.

48

"Here we are," Fern said at last, as Fluffy reached the edge of the maze. "Now which way do we go, girls?"

Rachel and Kirsty looked at each other in dismay. "This isn't the way we came *in*," Rachel said. "And I don't know the way back to the pot. Do you, Kirsty?"

Kirsty shook her head.

Fern looked worried. "But I have to get back to the pot!" she said.

"Oh!" Kirsty had an idea. "Rachel, what about looking in our magic bags?"

"Good idea," Rachel agreed.

Titania, the Fairy Queen, had given Rachel and Kirsty two special magic bags, for whenever they needed help. The girls took the bags with them everywhere.

Fluffy scrambled down the hedge to
the ground, and Rachel, Kirsty and Fern
climbed off his back. Kirsty opened her
rucksack and looked inside. One of the
magic bags was glowing with a silvery
light. "I wonder what's inside?" she said,
reaching in.

She pulled out a thin, green tube,
covered with sparkling gold stars.

"It looks like a *firework*," Rachel said. "That's not much use, is it?"

"It's a fairy firework!" said Fern excitedly. "We can shoot it into the sky, and my sisters will see it from the pot. Then they'll know we need help."

"But what about the goblins?" Rachel asked. "Won't they see it too, and know where we are?"

Fern looked serious. "We've got to take the risk," she said.

Kirsty stood the firework firmly in a patch of earth, then she and Rachel moved away from it. Fern hovered over the firework, her wings fluttering. She touched the top with her wand and quickly flew back to the girls.

Rachel and Kirsty held their breath as the tube caught light. Suddenly, with a loud fizz the whole firework shot upwards, trailing bright green sparks behind it. It climbed higher and higher into the sky, until it burst in a shower of emerald stars. The stars spelt out the words

They twinkled brightly in the darkening sky before fading away.

"We won't have to wait long," Fern said. "Help will come very soon."

Rachel and Kirsty wondered what was going to happen. How could the fairies come to their rescue? They weren't supposed to leave the clearing where the pot was, in case the goblins found them. Suddenly, there was a rustle of leaves behind them.

"Did you see that fairy firework?" shouted a loud voice. "It came from over there. Quick, before that fairy gets away again!"

Hedgehog Help

Rachel and Kirsty stared at each other in alarm. Fluffy looked scared too. The goblins were on their trail again!

"They're coming towards us," Rachel whispered as the voices got louder.

"Don't worry," Fern said, smiling. "My sisters will send help quickly."

Then Rachel spotted a line of golden
sparkles twinkling towards them
through the fruit trees. "What's that?"
she whispered.

"Is it goblin magic?" Kirsty asked
anxiously.

Fern shook her head. "They're
fireflies! My sisters must have sent them
to show us the way back to the pot."

Suddenly there was another shout
from inside the maze. "Look, what are
those lights over there?"

"The goblins have spotted the fireflies!" Rachel gasped.

"Quickly, Fluffy!" Fern said, as they climbed on to the squirrel's back again. "Follow the fireflies!"

The golden specks were dancing away through the trees. Fluffy scampered after them, just as the goblins dashed out of the maze.

"There's the fairy!" one of them shouted, pointing at Fern. "Stop that squirrel!"

"Come back!" the other roared as Fluffy ran off.

Rachel, Kirsty and Fern clung
to Fluffy's fur as the
squirrel zig-zagged
this way and that
to get away from
the goblins. Fluffy
scrambled up the
trunk of the nearest
tree. He was just
about to jump across
to the next, when someone
called to them from below.

"Hello!"

"Who's that?" Rachel asked.
She, Kirsty and Fern peered
down at the ground.
A hedgehog was
standing at the foot
of the apple tree.

"Hello," he called again. "The animals in the garden have heard that you're in trouble. We'd like to help."

"Oh, thank you," Fern called. Then she gasped as the two goblins appeared among the trees.

"Where's that squirrel gone?" one of them yelled.

Quickly Fluffy leaped across to the next apple tree. The goblins roared with rage and dashed forward. At that very moment, the hedgehog curled himself into a ball and rolled right into their path. Rachel thought he looked like a big, prickly football.

"OW!" both goblins howled. "My toes!"

Rachel and Kirsty couldn't help laughing as the goblins jumped around holding their feet. "Hooray for Hedgehog!" they shouted.

As Fluffy jumped from one fruit tree
to the next, the firefly lights behind
them began to go out.

"Hey! Who turned off the lights?"
wailed one of the goblins, still rubbing
his foot. "Which way are we supposed
to go?"

"How do I know, stupid?" snapped
the other goblin. Their voices were
getting fainter now as Fluffy hurried on.

"Thank you, fireflies," called Fern,
waving at the last few
specs of light.

"Now we need to
find a way to
the orchard wall.
We can't be far
from the pot
now."

"I can help you," a small voice whispered.

A fawn was standing at the bottom of the tree. Her golden brown coat was short and silky, and she stared up at them with big, brown eyes. "You mean you can show us the way?" Kirsty said. "Yes, I can," the deer nodded, twitching her little tail. "I can show you a short cut."

She trotted off through the trees on her long legs. Fluffy followed her, leaping from branch to branch above the little deer's head.

Rachel could hardly breathe for excitement. She was riding on a squirrel's back, being shown the way to the pot-at-the-end-of-the-rainbow by a fawn!

A few moments later they reached the brick wall which ran round the outside of the orchard. Fluffy leaped up to the top of the wall, and Rachel and Kirsty looked eagerly ahead of them. On the other side of the wall was a meadow, and beyond that a wood.

"Look!" Rachel shouted. "That's where the pot is!"

Flying High

"Thank you!" Kirsty and Rachel
called to the baby deer. She blinked
her long eyelashes at them, and
trotted away.

A blackbird with shiny, dark feathers
was sitting on the wall a little way
away. He hopped over to them, his
head on one side. "I'm here to take you

to the pot-at-the-end-of-the-rainbow,"
he chirped. "All aboard!"

Fluffy looked sad as Fern, Rachel and
Kirsty slid off his back and climbed on
to the blackbird. It was a tight squeeze,
and the feathers felt smooth and silky
after Fluffy's fur.

"Goodbye, Fluffy!" called Rachel,
and she blew him a kiss. She felt sad
to leave their new friend behind.

The blackbird soared into the air.

"Look for the big weeping willow tree," Rachel told the blackbird as he swooped across the meadow.

"I can't wait to see my sisters again," said Fern, sounding very excited.

The blackbird flew over the wood and landed in the clearing near the willow tree. Rachel, Kirsty and Fern jumped down on to the grass.

"Who's there?" croaked a stern voice.
A plump, green frog hopped out from
under the hanging branches of the tree.

"Bertram, it's me!" Fern
called. Quickly the fairy
waved her wand, and
Rachel and Kirsty
shot up to their
normal size again.
"Miss Fern!" Bertram
said joyfully. "You're back!"
"We followed the fireflies," Fern said,
giving the frog a hug. "Thank you for
sending them."

"We saw the firework in the sky,"
Bertram explained, "so we knew you
were in trouble. But you'll be safe
here," he went on. "The pot is hidden
under the tree."

Rachel and Kirsty hurried over and pulled aside the long branches. The pot-at-the-end-of-the-rainbow lay there on its side.

Suddenly a fountain of red, orange and yellow fairy dust whooshed out of the pot. Ruby, Amber and Saffron flew out, looking very excited. A big queen bee buzzed out behind them.

"Fern!" Ruby called. "You're safe! It's so good to see you!"

Rachel and Kirsty beamed as they watched the fairies hug each other. The air around them fizzed and popped with red flowers, green leaves, tiny, yellow butterflies and orange bubbles.

"We've really missed you," said Saffron. Beside her, the bee nudged her with a tiny feeler. "Oh, sorry, Queenie," said Saffron. "This is my sister, Fern."

Queenie buzzed, "Hello!"

"How did you get back so quickly?" asked Amber. "We only sent the fireflies a little while ago."

"Our woodland friends helped us," Fern said. She waved as the blackbird flew off. "Especially Fluffy the squirrel." She sighed. "It was a shame we had to leave him behind."

Ruby laughed. "Who's that then?" she asked, pointing at a tree on the other side of the clearing.

Rachel and Kirsty looked too. Fluffy
was peeping at them from behind the
tree trunk, looking very shy.

"Fluffy!" Fern flew over and hugged
him. "What are you doing here?"

"I was worried about you," Fluffy
explained shyly. "I wanted to make
sure you got back to the pot safely."

"Would you like to stay with us too?"
asked Amber. "You could live in the
willow tree, couldn't you?"

"Yes, *please*," squeaked Fluffy.

Ruby turned to Rachel and Kirsty.

"Thank you again," she said. "I don't know what we'd do without you!"

Fern fluttered lightly on to Rachel's shoulder. One of her wings brushed softly against Rachel's cheek, like a butterfly. "We'll see you again soon, won't we?"

"Yes, of course," Rachel promised.

"Only three more Rainbow Fairies left to find!" Kirsty added. She took Rachel's hand and they waved to the fairies, before running out of the clearing. "We'd better get back to your mum and dad, Rachel. They'll be wondering where we are."

"Good idea," Rachel laughed. "We'd better hurry back, before my dad eats all the picnic!"

Now it's time for Kirsty and Rachel to help...

Sky the Blue Fairy

Read on for a sneak peek...

"The water's really warm!" laughed
Rachel Walker. She was sitting on a rock,
swishing her toes in one of Rainspell
Island's deep, blue rock pools. Her friend
Kirsty Tate was looking for shells on the
rocks nearby.

"Mind you don't slip, Kirsty!" called Mrs
Tate. She was sitting further down the
beach with Mrs Walker.

"OK, Mum!" Kirsty yelled back. As she
looked down at her bare feet, a patch of
green seaweed began to move. There was
something blue and shiny underneath it.

"Rachel! Come over here," she shouted.

Rachel went over to Kirsty. "What is it?" she asked.

Kirsty pointed to the seaweed. "There's something blue under there," she said. "I wonder, could it be…"

"Sky the Blue Fairy?" Rachel said eagerly.

Jack Frost had banished the seven Rainbow Fairies from Fairyland with a magic spell…

Read Sky the Blue Fairy to find out what adventures are in store for Kirsty and Rachel!

Calling all parents, carers and teachers!
The Rainbow Magic fairies are here to help
your child enter the magical world of reading.
Whatever reading stage they are at, there's
a Rainbow Magic book for everyone!
Here is Lydia the Reading Fairy's guide to
supporting your child's journey at all levels.

(1) ## Starting Out
Our Rainbow Magic Beginner Readers are perfect for first-time readers who are just beginning to develop reading skills and confidence. Approved by teachers, they contain a full range of educational levelling, as well as lively full-colour illustrations.

(2) ## Developing Readers
Rainbow Magic Early Readers contain longer stories and wider vocabulary for building stamina and growing confidence. These are adaptations of our most popular Rainbow Magic stories, specially developed for younger readers in conjunction with an Early Years reading consultant, with full-colour illustrations.

(3) ## Going Solo
The Rainbow Magic chapter books - a mixture of series and one-off specials - contain accessible writing to encourage your child to venture into reading independently. These highly collectible and much-loved magical stories inspire a love of reading to last a lifetime.

www.rainbowmagicbooks.co.uk

"Rainbow Magic got my daughter reading chapter books. Great sparkly covers, cute fairies and traditional stories full of magic that she found impossible to put down" - Mother of Edie (6 years)

"Florence LOVES the Rainbow Magic books. She really enjoys reading now" - Mother of Florence (6 years)

The Rainbow Magic Reading Challenge

Well done, fairy friend – you have completed the book!
This book was worth 5 points.

See how far you have climbed on the
Reading Rainbow opposite.

The more books you read, the more points you will get,
and the closer you will be to becoming a Fairy Princess!

How to get your Reading Rainbow
1. Cut out the coin below
2. Go to the Rainbow Magic website
3. Download and print out your poster
4. Add your coin and climb up the Reading Rainbow!

There's all this and lots more at
www.rainbowmagicbooks.co.uk

You'll find activities, competitions, stories, a special
newsletter and complete profiles of all the
Rainbow Magic fairies. Find a fairy with your name!